Jonah

by Rachel Bonds

FOR PRODUCTION INQUIRIES

UNITED STATES AND CANADA
info@concordtheatricals.com
1-866-979-0447

UNITED KINGDOM AND EUROPE
licensing@concordtheatricals.co.uk
020-7054-7298

No one shall make any changes in this title(s) for the purpose of production. No part of this book may be reproduced, stored in a retrieval system, scanned, uploaded, or transmitted in any form, by any means, now known or yet to be invented, including mechanical, electronic, digital, photocopying, recording, videotaping, or otherwise, without the prior written permission of the publisher. No one shall share this title(s), or any part of this title(s), through any social media or file hosting websites.

For all inquiries regarding motion picture, television, online/digital and other media rights, please contact Concord Theatricals Corp.

MUSIC AND THIRD-PARTY MATERIALS USE NOTE

Licensees are solely responsible for obtaining formal written permission from copyright owners to use copyrighted music and/or other copyrighted third-party materials (e.g. artworks, logos) in the performance of this play and are strongly cautioned to do so. If no such permission is obtained by the licensee, then the licensee must use only original music and materials that the licensee owns and controls. Licensees are solely responsible and liable for clearances of all third-party copyrighted materials, including without limitation music, and shall indemnify the copyright owners of the play(s) and their licensing agent, Concord Theatricals Corp., against any costs, expenses, losses and liabilities arising from the use of such copyrighted third-party materials by licensees. For music, please contact the appropriate music licensing authority in your territory for the rights to any incidental music.

IMPORTANT BILLING AND CREDIT REQUIREMENTS

If you have obtained performance rights to this title, please refer to your licensing agreement for important billing and credit requirements.

JONAH was originally Produced in New York City by Roundabout Theatre Company (Scott Ellis, Acting Artistic Director; Sydney Beers, Managing Director) at the Harold and Miriam Steinberg Center for Theatre/Laura Pels Theatre on February 1, 2024. The production was directed by Danya Taymor, with sets by Wilson Chin, costumes by Kaye Voyce, lights by Amith Chandrashaker, sound by Kate Marvin, hair & makeup by Tommy Kurzman, illusions by Morgan Auld, voice and text coaching by Gigi Buffington, movement coordination by Tilly Evans-Krueger, and intimacy coordination by Ann James. The Production Stage Manager was Jennifer Rae Moore. The cast was as follows:

ANA . . . . Gabby Beans

JONAH . . . . Hagan Oliveras

DANNY . . . . Samuel Henry Levine

STEVEN . . . . John Zdrojeski

CHARACTERS

ANA – ages sixteen, eighteen to twenty-one, then later thirties/forty
JONAH – seventeen
DANNY – ages seventeen through early twenties
STEVEN – late thirties or early forties
And the offstage voice of Ana's **STEPFATHER**, middle-aged.

SETTING

A series of bedrooms, including: a boarding school dorm room, a bedroom in a house in the suburbs of Detroit, a college dorm room in Michigan, a bedroom at a remote writers' residency somewhere in the woods. The first two scenes take place outside the boarding school dorm. The setting there should feel only half-realized, half-imagined, a little fuzzy, still taking shape or coming into view. By the third scene, once they enter Ana's room, the sense of place can snap into focus.

TIME

The past and the present. But everything is slippery.

AUTHOR'S NOTES

Intimacy – This play requires intimacy choreography. It must be handled with sensitivity and intelligence. I suggest hiring an Intimacy Coordinator and including that person in as much of the rehearsal process as possible. I've built the play to take care of both the actors and the audience; it is of the utmost importance to me. So proceed with thoughtfulness, check in with one another frequently, and as the great Intimacy Coordinator Ann James says, "move at the speed of trust."

Casting – It is my great hope that this play can hold all different kinds of bodies and thus, stories. These characters could be played by actors of any race/ethnicity and the story can and should shift a bit depending on what each of these actors brings to the stage. As an artistic team entering the casting process, have the vital conversations about what each casting choice means for the story you're putting into the world and be mindful of what power dynamics are at play.

Language – The punctuation is key and will let you find the music of the play. Pauses are carefully built in. A slash (/) indicates an overlap in dialogue.

ACKNOWLEDGEMENTS

I want to thank the late, great SPACE on Ryder Farm, where I wrote most of the first draft of this play in one feverish week. Thank you to Jen Silverman, who read the first draft first and when I asked if it was something, said yes. Thank you to Sarah Gancher for her support in writing and in life. Thank you to Play Group for reading an early draft out loud on Zoom in the middle of a global pandemic. Thank you to Elna Baker and her piece "The Old Man on My Shoulder" for THIS AMERICAN LIFE Episode "But That's What Happened" for insight into Steven. Thank you to my family, without whom I could never have reached so far into the deep depths that this piece required.

*For everyone who
has ever felt
divided.*

JONAH. Hey wait up!

Hey! – Jesus you're walking fast, why are you walking so fast?

ANA. I have to be back in my room in ten minutes.

JONAH. Why?

ANA. And aren't you a day student?

JONAH. Yeah, but / I'm…

ANA. Because they check to make sure we're all in our rooms by nine.

JONAH. Oh, so where are you going?

ANA. To get something at the student center.

JONAH. What?

ANA. Why do you care?

JONAH. Can I walk with you?

ANA. Do what you want.

JONAH. What are you getting at the student center?

ANA. Why are you here so late?

JONAH. Charles King and I have a presentation for American History tomorrow, so we were working in his / dorm.

ANA. On what?

JONAH. Japanese internment camps.

I'm Jonah.

ANA. Ana.

JONAH. I know. You're from Detroit?

ANA. Why do you know that?

JONAH. Charles told me. Are you mad that I know that?

ANA. Goodbye.

JONAH. What are you getting in there?

ANA. *(Over her shoulder.)* Why do you care?! Candy!

(She goes to get candy. She comes back.)

JONAH. Ooh Sour Patch Kids. Those're the best.

ANA. Why are you still here?

JONAH. I'll walk you back to your dorm.

ANA. I don't need an escort.

JONAH. No, I know. But my car's back this way anyway and I don't want to walk by myself.

ANA. Why?

JONAH. Because there's bobcats around here. Did you know that? And rattlesnakes. Jesus Christ you walk fast.

ANA. Ms. Simons will fry my ass if I'm not in my room in two minutes.

JONAH. Oof, Ms. Simons is scary as shit, she's your dorm parent?

ANA. Yeah. Lucky me.

JONAH. Can I have one of those? I like the orange ones.

ANA. No. There are not rattlesnakes here.

JONAH. There are! I've seen them.

ANA. Where?

JONAH. Dead and squished on the road, but – I've seen them. There was one in our driveway once when I was a kid.

ANA. Dead?

JONAH. Yeah, my mom ran it over. Its guts were all over the gravel. Rattle was still intact, / though.

ANA. Eugh.

JONAH. I brought it in for Show & Tell.

ANA. With all the guts and shit?

JONAH. No, no, just the – rattle. Everyone was like, whaaaaaaaaa, Jonah, you are awesome.

ANA. Goodbye.

JONAH. I like you!

ANA. No you don't!

> *(She leaves him outside the dorm and goes up to her room, sits on her bed, and eats five Sour Patch Kids, one by one, contemplating. Then she crawls across the rug and peeks out the window. She stands up and looks down at him on the sidewalk. He waves. She lifts her shirt over her head and stares down at him, topless. Then pulls the shade.)*

^^^^^^^^^^^^^^

JONAH. Hey.

ANA. Hey.

Why are you out here?

JONAH. I'm a student monitor. One night / a week.

ANA. Not of this girl's dorm you're not.

JONAH. No – I monitor the computer lab on Tuesday nights. Are you going to get candy?

ANA. Why?

JONAH. Because I'll walk with you.

ANA. Aren't you supposed to be monitoring?

JONAH. No, I was done at eight.

ANA. Have you just been standing out here waiting for me?

JONAH. ...No.

ANA. Have you?

JONAH. I – don't know.

Why did you do that?

ANA. What?

JONAH. The other night. I didn't –. I don't want you to feel like you have to –.

ANA. I don't have to do anything. I do what I want.

JONAH. Okay. But. Why did you do that?

ANA. Because I wanted to.

JONAH. But why?

ANA. Did you have a problem with it?

JONAH. I –. No. Yes? I don't know! – I'm just trying to figure it out.

ANA. There's nothing to figure out.

JONAH. I'm just confused.

ANA. They're breasts. That's it. They're not some mysterious voodoo shit. You don't have to get all –stuttery about them.

JONAH. Okay. I –. Sorry. I. Misunderstood.

ANA. Are you a virgin?

JONAH. I – why?

ANA. It's okay if you are.

JONAH. ...I know.

ANA. Are you?

JONAH. I mean...yes.

ANA. Okay.

JONAH. Okay what?

ANA. So all you've been thinking about for the past week is my boobs.

JONAH. I mean...

ANA. Don't lie.

JONAH. You're seared in my memory now. You'll never be un-seared.

ANA. Hm.

JONAH. ...Are you a virgin?

ANA. ...

You can walk me to the student center. I have ten minutes.

JONAH. Okay.

JONAH. Oh, Christ – are you – God you walk so fucking fast you know that?

ANA. You take the Lord's name in vain a lot.

JONAH. Oh shit, are you really Christian? / I'm sorry.

ANA. No. I mean. I was raised Catholic, but –.

JONAH. But?

ANA. But I don't go to church anymore.

JONAH. Oh.

Do you still believe in God?

ANA. …I don't know.

…Do you?

JONAH. I –. I don't know. Sometimes I think I do, I mean I want to, and then…

ANA. What?

JONAH. Then I think it's all really silly shit we made up so we wouldn't be afraid and honestly, really, there's probably just black nothingness after we die.

ANA. …Yeah.

JONAH. Which, yeah…makes me afraid. So then I want to believe in heaven and seeing people I – yeah, that I miss, but then I know I just want that because it feels less scary than believing they're just black empty nothingness now.

ANA. But if they're nothingness then they don't feel pain anymore. Pain doesn't exist. Nothing exists. They don't care if they're nothingness. They're free from all that.

JONAH. That's true.

ANA. Who do you miss?

JONAH. Uhhh. My mom's dead, so.

ANA. / Oh.

JONAH. Wait, so, did you have to do confession and all that?

ANA. Yes.

JONAH. Eugh.

ANA. What?

JONAH. That's so weird.

ANA. I mean, yeah, / it's...

JONAH. With the man behind the curtain listening to you talk about jerking off and everything you did wrong and everything?

ANA. I didn't talk about that.

JONAH. No, no, of course you didn't, but...that's what I'd be in there for. Like every few hours, I'd have to go in the box with the man to talk about masturbating. That would be so awful, I'm glad I'm not Catholic.

ANA. Every few hours?

JONAH. I mean, not every few hours, but – a lot.

ANA. Girls masturbate too. You know that right?

JONAH. I –. I mean, I guess I know that but I don't really know it.

ANA. We do.

JONAH. A lot?

ANA. Yeah.

JONAH. ...You. Do?

ANA. Yeah.

JONAH. A lot?

ANA. I mean...what else is there to do around here?

(*He laughs.*)

JONAH. Aw man.

ANA. What?

JONAH. I like you.

ANA. I have to go. I'm gonna be late for roll call.

JONAH. I don't want you to.

ANA. Well I'll –. "Wave" at you from my window.

JONAH. You don't have to do that.

ANA. I do what I want, Jonah.

JONAH. ...Okay.

  I really like you.

ANA. Shut up.

^^^^^^^^^^

ANA. You have to be quiet.

JONAH. I will.

ANA. Really quiet. Ms. Simons hears everything. Every breath we take.

JONAH. Oh God.

ANA. She does.

JONAH. Okay.

ANA. She's like a bat. A supersonic-hearing bat.

JONAH. I believe you.

ANA. Quiet.

(He holds up his hands in acceptance.)

JONAH. I like your room.

ANA. Shut up.

JONAH. *(Looking at a photo.)* I do! It's nice.

(He picks up the photo.)

Is this your mom?

ANA. Yeah. And my two sisters.

JONAH. All girls.

ANA. All girls. I'm the baby.

JONAH. You look so much like her. I mean, you all do. But YOU really do.

ANA. I know. Everyone says I look exactly like she did.

JONAH. I wish I looked like my mom.

ANA. You must a little.

JONAH. I mean, sure. But I look way more like my dad. And he's kind of weird-looking, so – oh well for me!

ANA. Do you want to sit down?

JONAH. Uhh. Where?

ANA. On the bed, weirdo.

JONAH. Uhhhh that's gonna...mm, okay, / yeah.

ANA. You're so weird.

JONAH. What are you gonna do?

ANA. I am also going to sit down.

JONAH. Where?

ANA. On the bed.

JONAH. Mm okay.

ANA. Okay?

JONAH. Yeah yeah yeah yeah. The world inside me is lighting itself on fire, but yeah.

ANA. What?!

JONAH. And I might die, but, yeah, go ahead and sit next to me on your bed. I'm sorry – I think I'm crazy.

ANA. Why?

JONAH. You don't feel this way?

ANA. I mean –

JONAH. Sex is everywhere. Literally everywhere. Everything is sex.

ANA. Like what?

JONAH. Everything. Everything! I'll see, like, the corner of the desk in front of me in English and it'll somehow make me think of a nipple and then –. Or we'll be stretching for soccer and I'm just staring at someone's – anyone's! – calf muscle and then all of a sudden – or or or my desk lamp! At home! Sort of looks like a boob and then, – or! God! Just the way the dry erase marker touches the dry erase board is like somehow – something about *that*, I don't even know what?! – and what is wrong with me, am I crazy?

ANA. No.

JONAH. Do you think these things?

ANA. I – yeah, sometimes. It's different.

JONAH. How?

ANA. Uhhh. For me there's usually a story involved.

JONAH. What do you mean, like…

ANA. Like someone is showing up at my door. And he's like, wet from being in the pouring rain. And his face is all like desperate and sad and I open the door, and I'm like Colin?, and he's like, / I didn't get on the flight. Shut up –

JONAH. Colin?

ANA. And I'm like, What are you –? – and he's like – I didn't get on the flight. I didn't get on the flight. I just got back in my car and came straight here because I just have to tell you that I'm completely in love with you. And I'm sorry. And I know you don't love me back, I know that, and that's okay, it's totally okay, but I just needed to tell you or I'd go crazy, and I'm like, Colin, Colin, Colin: I do love you. I've only ever loved you, since we were ten years old, I've been in love with you since the minute I saw you, and then, like, he rushes into the room and takes my face and he kisses me and like, I think we have sex?

JONAH. Whoa, but is this / like –

ANA. But it's not so much about all the body parts but about the feelings?

JONAH. Wait, but is Colin a real person?

ANA. No! That's – not the point. Or I'll be like, okay: I'm older and I'm on a job somewhere, I'm a journalist, and this guy who works with me is a photographer – and we've been working together for a long time as friends, but then one night he knocks on my door really late, and we're in some weird hotel wherever we're doing the story, and it's kind of dangerous where we are, like I've already got a nasty wound from where a bullet grazed my arm, and / he knocks on my door –

JONAH. *(Wincing.)* You have a gunshot wound?!

ANA. Yes! Shut up! And he's like hi, and I'm like, hi, and then he comes in the room and is like, I just want you to know I've asked to be reassigned – so I'll be heading out to Madrid in the morning, and I'm like, Wait, why?!, and he's like, It's just better for everyone, and I'm like, What?! No it's not!!, and he's like, Well it's better for me, and I'm like, Why?! and then he just yells out, Because I'm falling in love with you, Ana! I'm in love with you! And then we stare at each other for a moment, and we kiss, like, the best – like the best, most full, most passionate kiss ever, and then I guess we have sex.

JONAH. You guess?

ANA. But that part's not really detailed, it's more about the – the first part. And then there's this other one when I'm at camp, like I'm a camp counselor out in the woods in the middle of nowhere, and all the kids are asleep and I'm hanging out with the other counselors around a campfire, and this one guy who's been totally standoffish all summer, like quiet and always by himself, he never hangs out except for some reason he is tonight, and everyone thinks he's hiding something, like something sad and bad from his past, and he keeps staring at me through the smoke and everything, and I'm like, I'm gonna go swim across the lake, does anyone want to come?, and he's like, I'll come. So we swim out toward the middle of the lake, but I'm a better swimmer than he is, and he's like, Wait up!, but I just laugh and keep going, but then he starts struggling to breathe, like – bad, so I have to grab him and swim with him all the way to the opposite bank, and pull him out of the water, and he's coughing and wheezing and stuff – and we sit on the rocks together until his breath comes back to normal, and like silently watch the fire flickering on the other side of the lake. And then he breaks the silence to say: What am I gonna do, Ana? And I'm like, I don't know, take some swim lessons? And he laughs, but then he's like, I mean what am I gonna do about being completely fucking in love with you? And then he looks up at me, and he's crying a little bit, and then I'm crying a little bit, and then we kiss, and it's like, everything just explodes in our hearts, and I take off my bathing suit top and then we have sex. Like on the rocks. While we're both kind of crying.

JONAH. Whoa.

ANA. Yeah.

JONAH. Whoa.

ANA. Yeah.

JONAH. Yours are so much better than mine. Mine's just like, Oh man, I'm touching a butt.

(She laughs.)

But that's because I don't really know anything about anything.

ANA. I don't know anything either.

JONAH. Yes you do.

ANA. No.

JONAH. Or, I thought – don't you?

ANA. No, not about – real stuff.

JONAH. What do you mean?

ANA. I mean I've kissed people before but, like, that's it.

JONAH. Oh. Man. Really?

ANA. Yeah. And they weren't like – serious making out or anything.

JONAH. Really?

ANA. Yes. Why are you so surprised?

JONAH. Because! Because I thought you – the way you were talking to me that day about me being a virgin and everything, I thought –

ANA. Nope.

JONAH. So you are too?

ANA. Yeah.

JONAH. Oh. Oh.

...Who'd you kiss? Was it someone named Colin?

ANA. *(Swatting at him, laughing.)* No! No. Just – some people where I'm from. From my old school.

JONAH. Okay.

ANA. But people always...

(She shakes her head.)

JONAH. What?

ANA. People always think I'm slutty or something because... I don't know – I guess something about me makes them think that.

JONAH. I don't think that.

ANA. You did! You did think that!

JONAH. No, I didn't think slutty! I thought "experienced." I thought you had done things, I / don't know.

ANA. Yeah, but…everyone thinks that. Everyone thought that at my old school, they were always like, Ooh all the boys must be up on her!

JONAH. Oh no.

ANA. When the whole time, I'm just like, I was like, don't look at me, don't look at me, don't look at me. If I saw anyone looking at me, I crossed the street, or I went in the bathroom. I hate being looked at like that.

JONAH. I'm sorry. Is that why you…?

ANA. What?

JONAH. Is that why you came here?

ANA. I mean…partly. I think my mom wanted me to be in a better school, and like, have more opportunities. She knew I was miserable. Then someone told her about this place, so we applied. And then they offered me a full scholarship, so…

JONAH. Wow. Wow. Well, she sounds pretty cool.

ANA. My mom? Yeah, she's awesome. I really miss her.

JONAH. …Yeah totally.

Well, I'm sorry I assumed something about you. That was shitty of me.

ANA. It's okay.

JONAH. I just assume everyone is more experienced than me, so –

ANA. So how much have you – wait, you were with Danielle though, weren't you?

JONAH. Kinda. I mean, we've made out, but.

ANA. Okay. So. Who else did you kiss?

JONAH. Uhhhhhh, Tricia Anderson in sixth grade, Crystal Barnett in eighth grade, *and* in ninth grade, actually, when we, uh, rekindled our love for a week, and then Danielle.

ANA. Just kissing?

JONAH. Just kissing.

ANA. Really?

JONAH. I mean...I guess Danielle and I did a little – touching, but not...it was all over the clothing and not – I mean her parents were always home. Always. So. And I don't know...

ANA. What?

JONAH. I don't think either of us even liked each other that much, it was just – something we both thought we were supposed to do?

ANA. Yeah.

JONAH. I mean, I know I didn't like her. I didn't. Not really. And we were only together for a few weeks and then my mom died, so I didn't, uhhhhhhh –. Yeah, then I really didn't want to do anything with anyone – like at *all* ever *again*, so. / Yeahhhhh.

ANA. Yeah.

JONAH. *(Wiping his eyes quickly.)* Uhhhhhhhhhhh, and now you know everything I've ever done!, so – Ohmygod I'm sorry, I don't know why I'm crying.

ANA. That's okay.

JONAH. *(Wiping his eyes fervently.)* Oh. God. Jesus Christ. Sorry.

ANA. It's okay.

JONAH. Sorry Sorry / Sorry.

ANA. Stop, it's okay.

JONAH. Auuuughh go back inside my eyes, tears! Go back inside my eyes! Auuughh sorry!

> *(He holds his hands over his eyes for a moment trying to keep it all in, but he can't,*

and he gives over to it for a moment, his body shaking silently. She watches him for a moment. She puts her hand on his back.)

ANA. Jonah.

(He just shakes his head, hands still over his face, shaking.)

I'm just going to sit here.

JONAH. Okay.

ANA. I'm just going to sit next to you.

JONAH. Okay.

ANA. And put my hand on your back. Don't freak out.

JONAH. *(Laugh-crying.)* Okay, I'll – I'll try!

ANA. I'm just going to be next to you.

JONAH. ...Okay.

(He laughs, and cries, his hands still over his face.)

(They sit next to each other. He cries. She holds her hand on his back. He wipes his eyes.)

(He looks at her. She looks at him. She looks away. He looks away. They sit next to each other.)

^^^^^^^^^^

ANA. Vivian said she heard us the other night.

JONAH. What'd she hear?

ANA. Just that I was talking to someone.

JONAH. Does she know it was me?

ANA. No, I told her I was on the phone with my cousin.

JONAH. Okay.

ANA. I mean I also told her to stop being such a little fucking snoop.

JONAH. Whoa, okay.

ANA. But yeah, you better be quiet.

JONAH. *(Whispering.)* I'll be quiet.

Your room still looks nice.

ANA. Thanks.

(A pause.)

JONAH. Um.

So.

Sorry I had a nervous breakdown on your bed.

ANA. That's okay.

JONAH. I don't know what happened.

ANA. I mean...

JONAH. I was just – you somehow make me feel like I can say literally everything inside of me and then that opened the storm door I guess and then – all the bad stuff, it came for me.

ANA. I liked it.

JONAH. You liked it?

ANA. I mean, I like that you tell me things. And that you drowned me in your tears.

JONAH. Oh Jesus.

ANA. I'm messing with you, I'm / messing.

JONAH. Euugh. Okay.

Um. How was your day?

ANA. Okay.

JONAH. What happened?

ANA. Mmmm Jamie fell asleep in Algebra 2 and Ms. Nelson threw a notebook at his head.

JONAH. Ahahaha, did he wake up?

ANA. No! He was dead asleep. I feel bad for him, I think he's – he told me he takes care of his younger sisters while his mom's at work at night, / so.

JONAH. Yeah she's a nurse.

ANA. He's probably just really tired. I feel like the teachers here don't get that.

JONAH. Really? I think they do.

ANA. I think they all grew up super privileged and never had to take care of anyone in their family and they just wanna teach here because they're too afraid of the public schools.

JONAH. Not all of them are like that.

ANA. Jonah.

JONAH. And you don't know what their families are like.

ANA. Mm, I can guess.

Though Ms. Nelson did ask me if I was okay after class today.

JONAH. Why?

ANA. She said I looked like I was somewhere else.

JONAH. Where were you?

ANA. Uhhhhh I don't know. Definitely not thinking about solving for x.

JONAH. What were you thinking about?

(She shoves him.)

What?!

ANA. *(Laughing.)* Stop!

JONAH. *(Laughing.)* What?! – I just asked you a simple question!

ANA. *(Shoving him.)* Shut up!

JONAH. Ow! I just asked you a question, you don't have to hit me, God! You're mean.

ANA. I know.

JONAH. You wanna know what my dad said tonight at dinner?

ANA. Yeah.

JONAH. He was like "What's happening with you bud, do you want to go back to that therapist?" and I was like, "No?! – What? Why?," and he's like, "I was reading this thing that said we're gonna re-grieve for Mom every time something major happens," and I was like, "Okayyy," and he was like, "So did something major happen?"

ANA. Oh.

JONAH. "You seem really distracted lately, like something's going on." And I just, I mean I love him, I do, but all I wanted was for him to shut up and go drink in his room so I could come here and talk to you, did you drug me?

ANA. *(Smiling.)* What?!

JONAH. Or did you put a spell on me or something the other night? / Are you a magical being?

ANA. *(Laughing.)* Maybe.

Maybe.

...Did something major happen?

JONAH. Uhhhh. I mean. My heart exploded in your bed right in front of you, so...

ANA. So.

JONAH. So. What were you thinking about in Ms. Nelson's class?

(She gives him a look.)

What?

ANA. *(A small shove.)* Don't.

JONAH. Whaaaat? Again, I'm just asking a simple question, it just requires a simple / answer.

ANA. *(Another shove.)* You know.

JONAH. What?! I don't know, what are you thinking / about?

ANA. *(Another shove.)* Yes you do know!

JONAH. No I don't! Ow! Hey!

(She kisses him. He kisses her back. A pause.)

(Eyes still closed.) ...Oooooohhkay.

ANA. What?

JONAH. *(Opening his eyes.)* Now I'm gonna fail out of school.

(She laughs.)

> *(They kiss.)*

JONAH. Okay.

> *(They kiss again. And again.)*

Okay.

> *(He has an erection.)*

Oh god. Sorry – / don't –.

ANA. It's –

JONAH. I'm sorry.

> *(He jumps away and lies face down on her bed.)*

Give me a minute, it'll go away.

ANA. Jonah.

JONAH. Euughhh centipedes tadpoles slugs / slugs slugs centipedes centipedes

ANA. What are you doing?!

JONAH. Help me think of other gross stuff that's gross – slugs slugs catfood leeches snot slugs SLUGS!

ANA. It's okay Jonah.

JONAH. No, I don't want to be creepy.

ANA. You're not creepy.

JONAH. *(Burying his head.)* Yes I am. Don't look at me. Just – move over there.

ANA. Jonah.

JONAH. No! Don't! – touch me! You'll make it worse.

ANA. Okay!, but. I'm just saying it's / okay.

JONAH. I don't want to be weird and I just want you to feel okay and safe and my whole body is basically an alien colony, I have been colonized by sex aliens and I'm sorry.

ANA. Jonah. Here. Come here.

JONAH. Why?

ANA. Because I want you to.

(He peeks at her, then wriggles backward out of the bed and slides himself down and over to her. They look in each other's eyes. She kisses him.)

JONAH. Okay... I have to tell you – if you –

(She kisses him again.)

...If you keep doing that, it's just – it's –

ANA. I know.

(She kisses him again. Strongly. He pulls away.)

JONAH. I'm – you have to tell me if you don't feel safe.

ANA. I will.

JONAH. Okay? Are you okay?

ANA. I'm okay.

JONAH. Okay.

(They kiss. More and more.)

ANA. I don't think I want to have sex yet.

JONAH. No, no, we don't have to, we don't have to.

ANA. Okay. But I want to do other stuff?

JONAH. Okay.

ANA. Okay.

JONAH. Okay. Just – tell me. What to do.

ANA. Okay. Here.

JONAH. What?

ANA. You can touch a butt. Your fantasy is coming true.

(She puts his hands on her butt. He laughs.)

JONAH. Wow.

All my fantasies are coming true.

ANA. Yeah.

JONAH. Um okay, here.

ANA. What?

JONAH. Um. Here.

(He takes her hands and holds them and looks down at them for a moment and then looks up at her dramatically.)

I didn't get on the flight.

ANA. Okay, stop!

JONAH. I didn't get on the flight.

ANA. Don't make fun / of me!

JONAH. I didn't get on the flight, because I couldn't – I can't – I can't stop thinking about you. I can't stop thinking about you, I haven't stopped thinking about you since the moment I saw you, I just, I think you are the most interesting, most beautiful person I've ever seen, and all I want is to talk to you and make you laugh and make you feel really good, and I have no idea what I'm doing, I don't know what I'm doing, Ana, I have no idea what I'm doing, I don't know what to do at all except get in my car and come over here and sneak into your dorm room and probably get expelled and talk to you until it's morning and that's all I want to do forever, except now that you introduced touching you, now

I also want to do that forever, so just tell me what to do because I'm afraid, I'm afraid, I mean I know, I know, I know that Ana, I, Ana, I –

(He holds her face in his hands.)

Ana.

(He flinches.)

Ana.

(He flinches.)

Ana.

(The door flies open, darkness beyond.)

Ana.

(He disappears backward through the door, sucked into the darkness.)

*(**DANNY** appears in the open doorway.)*

DANNY. Ana.

ANA. Yeah?

DANNY. What are you doing?

ANA. Nothing. Thinking.

DANNY. ...I've been standing here for like ten minutes.

ANA. No you haven't.

DANNY. What are you thinking about?

ANA. Something for school.

What?

DANNY. Where'd you get it?

ANA. What?

DANNY. Whatever you're on right now.

ANA. I'm not on anything.

DANNY. You're on a whole other planet. Who gave it to
    you?

ANA. I'm not high.

DANNY. Was it that kid at the 7-11 that you like?

ANA. Kevin? I don't like him.

DANNY. Are you gonna share?

ANA. I'm not high.

DANNY. Whatever.

ANA. Whatever.

DANNY. Dad's freaking out downstairs. He wants you to
    help James with his math.

ANA. Right now?

DANNY. Yup.

ANA. Euuuuggghhhhhh. 'Kay.

>   *(She gets up off the bed.)*

DANNY. Because apparently I'm "fucking retarded," / so.

ANA. Stop. Did he say that?

DANNY. Eh.

ANA. Fuck him.

DANNY. Yup.

    ...Hey, I saw you talking to him, though. Kevin.

ANA. I mean, I talk to him when I buy something at 7-11
    and he's working there, it'd be weird not to –

DANNY. I saw you talking to him in the parking lot.

ANA. Were you spying on me?

DANNY. No, I was getting gas and I saw you.

ANA. 'Kay, well good for you.

DANNY. I hope you're using condoms.

ANA. Fuck off.

DANNY. Hey!

ANA. We were talking about something for school.

DANNY. What thing?

ANA. Just – an essay we have to write for English.

DANNY. What is it?

ANA. Just this – we read *The Great Gatsby* and now we have to write our own – about our own "American dream."

DANNY. Hh. What's yours about?

ANA. Uhhh getting into college and getting the fuck out of here.

    (He nods.)

DANNY. Right.

    Hey, though. Just be careful.

ANA. About what?

DANNY. Just – I heard some stuff.

ANA. Why are you getting all red?

DANNY. I'm not – I just heard some stuff. I heard Kevin plays rough.

ANA. Who'd you hear that from?

DANNY. From April. I heard he kinda fucked her up, so / just –

ANA. April is always saying shit –

DANNY. Just be careful is all I'm saying. Okay?

(He looks at her. She looks at him. A tiny pause, a moment of confusion.)

ANA. …Okay.

Why are you blushing?

(She comes toward him.)

DANNY. I'm not – don't –

(She reaches toward his face.)

ANA. *(Reaching toward his face playfully.)* Yes you are! – you're / seriously –

DANNY. Stop, I'm – / not –

ANA. All red – / you're –

DANNY. *(Batting her away.)* No, I'm not, stop!

ANA. Yes you are, you're like bright *red* –

(He leans toward her – a sudden, different kind of closeness. It's strange but there's also some real heat there. They both feel it. It's confusing.)

…Danny.

DANNY. I, um –.

*(He touches a lock of her hair. Ana's **STEPFATHER** calls out from somewhere inside the house.)*

STEPFATHER. *(From offstage.)* Hey!

(They jump apart.)

Hello?! Can you please help James, for Chrissakes?! – He's a kid, he shouldn't be cleaning up after you two.

Danny, get your useless fucking ass down here and pick up these dishes!

DANNY. *(Yelling down.)* Yes sir!

STEPFATHER. *(From offstage.)* And Ana?! I better see you down here in two minutes for this homework, no more fucking around!

> *(She closes her eyes for a moment. **DANNY** watches her. She opens them again. They look at each other.)*
>
> *(**DANNY** disappears back through the door.)*

^^^^^^^^^^

JONAH. Hey.

ANA. Hi.

JONAH. Hey.

ANA. You shouldn't be here.

JONAH. I'm so sorry.

ANA. Ms. Simons is already super pissed, so you / should go.

JONAH. She is? – What happened?

ANA. You should go.

JONAH. Ana.

ANA. I waited for you.

JONAH. I know.

ANA. I waited for like – / almost two hours.

JONAH. I know, I'm so sorry.

ANA. Outside, in the – in the fucking woods, / just.

JONAH. Oh god, I know, I'm.

ANA. In the fucking woods! / I felt like a fucking idiot!

JONAH. I know. I'm. If I could explain to you the, the
– how much / I hate myself right now –

ANA. Do you not have a phone all of a sudden? / You text
me nonstop all day long every day and then – all of a
sudden, just –

JONAH. I left my phone in my car, and – I know, it died
in my car –

ANA. Nothing?! So you can't go out to your car and get
your fucking phone and plug it into the fucking wall
you fucking asshole fuck?

JONAH. Ana.

ANA. I was just out there, like – barely wearing clothes, / feeling like a fucking idiot,

JONAH. Oh Ana.

ANA. And then Simons saw me sneaking back in, / so.

JONAH. Oh shit –

ANA. And now she's calling my mother in the morning, and you know I could lose my scholarship, you / know that –

JONAH. Oh God, I'm so sorry.

ANA. I should never, never, never have trusted you.

JONAH. Don't say that. Please don't say that.

ANA. Why are you soaking wet?

JONAH. It's – I –

ANA. Don't drip all over all my stuff.

> *(She throws a towel at him. He catches it. He holds it but doesn't use it.)*

JONAH. Hey.

Seriously, I'm sorry.

I was with my dad.

> *(He laughs a short laugh, and covers his face for a moment, then uncovers it.)*

He, uh – I guess he came in wasted for a meeting? I mean, I know he drinks in his room after dinner and stuff but I didn't think he was doing it during *the day* – but I guess he is! So they suspended him and he called me crying to come pick him up and – it just took a while to get him home. And that's where I was, and I'm so sorry, I should have texted you, but my phone died and I left it in the car when I was trying to get him inside, and...yeah.

(She walks over to him.)

He was so drunk, I've / never...

ANA. Yeah.

JONAH. I mean, he peed on himself. At work. So I had to – I literally had to pick him up, like carry him, and put him in the shower with all his clothes on.

ANA. That's good. That's what you / should do.

JONAH. Which is why I'm all wet.

Is Ms. Simons really going to call your mom?

ANA. That's what she said.

JONAH. What about your scholarship?

ANA. I don't know! I don't know. I have two counts against me already, she said, so...they might kick me out. Wanna move to Detroit?

JONAH. Yes.

ANA. To a shitty suburb of Detroit?

JONAH. Yes.

ANA. No you don't.

JONAH. I would literally live inside the sewer if you wanted me to. And I would definitely go to the shitty suburbs of Detroit, I would go there in a heartbeat.

ANA. You'd have to live in the basement. My mom would never let you into my room.

JONAH. Great. I love basements.

ANA. ...I'm sorry I called you a fucking asshole fuck.

JONAH. That's okay.

ANA. God, Jonah, here.

(She takes the towel and rubs his hair, rubs his face, she tries to dry him off, and it's kind, and it's awkward, and they laugh.)

JONAH. Ow.

ANA. Shh, I'm – helping.

JONAH. *(Wincing as she playfully dries him off.)* Yeah yeah, okay thank you.

ANA. *(Roughly drying him off.)* There you go.

JONAH. *(Grabbing the towel.)* Ow. Okay. Thank you. Thanks so much.

ANA. Here, though, you should – you should take this off, you're soaked.

(She takes off his shirt.)

JONAH. ...Okay.

Uh.

ANA. And those.

JONAH. Uhh.

Are you sure?

ANA. Yes.

JONAH. Are you sure?

ANA. Yes.

(He takes off his shoes and pants.)

(She takes a step toward him. She takes off her shirt and pajama shorts.)

(They stand with each other in their underwear for a moment.)

JONAH. Hi.

ANA. Hi.

(She leaps at him into a kiss, a long, full, super passionate, fucking amazing kiss, throwing him up against the door.)

(They pull away a small amount, he holds her face, she holds him.)

JONAH. Tell me what to do.

ANA. I don't know.

JONAH. Tell me what to do.

ANA. I don't know.

JONAH. Because I am falling completely fucking in love with you, Ana, tell me what to do –

(They kiss again and again and again.)

ANA. I want to.

JONAH. Are you sure?

ANA. I want to.

JONAH. You're sure?

ANA. Yes.

JONAH. Okay, are you okay?

ANA. Yes.

(He flinches.)

JONAH. Okay?

(He flinches.)

Okay?

(He flinches.)

Okay?

> (*He flinches.*)

Okay?

> (*The door flies open. Darkness beyond. He is swallowed into the darkness.*)
>
> (**DANNY** *appears in the doorway.*)
>
> (**ANA** *grabs the towel and quickly wraps it around herself.*)

ANA. Hey – what are you – excuse me.

DANNY. Oh, shit, sorry.

ANA. Goodbye.

DANNY. Well why'd you have the door wide open?

ANA. I was about to close it, why are you looking in my room?

DANNY. I need a phone charger.

ANA. Why?

DANNY. Mine died or something, it's all / – not charging anymore.

ANA. Well – eugh – here.

> (*She pulls hers out of the wall and tosses it to him.*)

DANNY. Thanks.

> (*He grabs it with one arm, the other arm strangely frozen by his side, curled up against his body.*)

ANA. What's wrong with your arm?

DANNY. Eh I fucked it up at work or something.

ANA. Doing what?

DANNY. Just – twisted it in a weird way, it's just – sprained or something.

ANA. Do you want an ACE bandage, gimpy?

DANNY. Do you have one?

ANA. Yeah, I think – hold on – somewhere in / here –

(She rifles through her top drawer, pulling out underwear and bras as she searches. He picks up a pair of underwear.)

DANNY. Do these have Minnie Mouse on them?!

ANA. Shut up. Here, gimp.

(She hands him the ACE bandage.)

DANNY. Ooh, Minnie.

ANA. Shut up.

DANNY. What is she doing?

ANA. *(Grabbing them from him.)* I don't know.

DANNY. Jumping through a field of hearts?

ANA. *(Burying them in the drawer.)* Shut the fuck up.

DANNY. Hey now.

ANA. Seriously, stop.

DANNY. I'm sorry.

ANA. No you're not.

DANNY. I am. Can – will you just do this for me?

ANA. God you're helpless.

DANNY. What?

ANA. Fine fine.

(She takes the ACE bandage.)

Give me your arm, gimpy –

DANNY. Ow ow ow ow ow –

ANA. Sorry sorry, give me your, / here.

DANNY. Ow ow ow fuck fuck.

(She pauses. Looking at him.)

ANA. You okay?

DANNY. *(His eyes closed, nodding.)* Augh, yes.

(She examines his arm.)

ANA. This is bad, Danny.

DANNY. ...Eh...

ANA. It's pretty swollen, / it's –

DANNY. Yeah, it's. Ow ow.

ANA. Sorry sorry.

DANNY. *(Wincing.)* Mm *augh.*

(She finishes wrapping his hand/wrist. She holds it, staring down at it. They are quiet for a moment.)

ANA. ...Did he find out you were ditching school?

DANNY. ...I don't know.

ANA. *(Looking up at him.)* Danny.

DANNY. It was mostly because I scratched up the car. I mean, it's my car, I mean, it almost is, I'm almost done paying him for it, so I don't know why he's so...

ANA. Yeah.

DANNY. But it's fine...it's... / it'll heal.

ANA. No it's not.

> *(He shrugs and shakes his head.)*

Danny. It's not.

> *(He looks up at her.)*

DANNY. Sure... But what do we do about it?

ANA. I don't know, but we have to do something.

> *(He nods. He looks at her.)*

> *(She looks at him.)*

> *(He rubs his head into her neck. She rubs hers into his. They giggle. Heat grows. It feels both good and not good; it is something in-between.)*

> *(She pulls away.)*

We –. Danny.

DANNY. Can I –?

ANA. What?

DANNY. See you?

ANA. Uhhh...

DANNY. Please?

ANA. ...Okay, just – quick, okay? And just looking.

DANNY. Okay.

ANA. Okay.

> *(She shuts the door and turns back to him, opening her towel. He looks at her.)*

> *(The door flies open. He disappears into the dark hallway. **ANA** quickly gets dressed.)*

^^^^^^^^^^

*(**ANA** sits on her bed. **DANNY** in the doorway.)*

DANNY. Are you okay?

ANA. Yeah. That was a bad one.

DANNY. It was, uhh...yeah. Did James wake / up –

ANA. He's still asleep, I checked.

DANNY. Why didn't you lock the door?

ANA. He took the lock off.

DANNY. Fucker.

(She peers into the hallway.)

ANA. Is he still...

DANNY. He left.

ANA. 'Kay.

DANNY. Said he'd be back in a few days maybe.

ANA. Where'd he go?

DANNY. *(Shrugging.)* Some business thing he said. Probably just going to fuck off at the casino. But whatever, he's gone. He's gone.

(She visibly releases something inside herself. He moves slowly over to lower himself onto the bed.)

(She closes the door.)

ANA. Your leg?

DANNY. Yeah, fucked up my leg.

ANA. I heard a crash, like a – / loud –

DANNY. Yeah, I broke that fucking – display case thing, shit's in a million pieces. We should vacuum before James gets up.

ANA. He pushed you?

DANNY. Uh, went at me with a chair this time, the fucker.

 (Winces.)

/ Augh.

ANA. God, Danny, we have / to –

DANNY. What? What are we gonna do?

ANA. Tell someone.

DANNY. And all get put in foster care? So strangers can fuck us up? Fuck that shit, fuck that.

ANA. But we could, I don't know, tell a teacher or or – there's this lady from my old church that I used to be really close / with – or –

DANNY. Yeah, and then they split us up and put us in foster care. And then some dirty old asshole is gonna try to mess with you. That's what happens in foster care. So / let's just –

ANA. My English teacher, though, she likes me, I feel like she would know how to / help.

DANNY. That's nice for you then.

ANA. Danny.

DANNY. But we need to stay together.

ANA. ...Right.

DANNY. Don't you want to stay together?

ANA. I'm – yeah. Yeah.

DANNY. So then we have to figure this shit out on our own. I'm gonna figure it out. So don't go saying anything to anyone.

ANA. Okay.

(He shakes his head, rubs his eyes, adjusts his leg.)

DANNY. *(Wincing in pain.)* Aughh fuck.

ANA. Can I see?

DANNY. I don't know how bad it is. I'm afraid to look.

ANA. Okay.

DANNY. Might be pretty gross.

ANA. Just let me see it.

DANNY. Might be bloody and shit, I / don't know.

ANA. Just show me.

(He pauses for a moment, then lowers his jeans to his knees, turns his head away.)

(She looks. She touches his leg gently.)

It's not bleeding.

DANNY. 'Kay.

ANA. But we should put ice on it.

DANNY. *(Nodding.)* 'Kay.

ANA. I'm gonna go get some ice, okay?

DANNY. WAIT – Can you, um. Just, first – Can you just do that thing to my head you did last time?

ANA. Oh...sure. Here.

(She goes to him.)

> *(She holds his head and rubs her thumbs slowly on his temples. He closes his eyes.)*

ANA. Just – try to breathe.

DANNY. Yeah.

ANA. 'Kay?

DANNY. Yeah.

ANA. Breathe, Danny.

DANNY. *(Nodding, his eyes filling behind his lids.)* ...'Kay.

ANA. Just breathe.

> *(He nods silently, wipes tears away from his closed eyes.)*

Breathe.

DANNY. 'Kay.

> *(She holds his head gently. He keeps his eyes closed.)*

God.

ANA. What?

DANNY. You're just... Really good at calming me down.

> *(He opens his eyes. He reaches out and holds a lock of her hair.)*

I think you're really pretty.

ANA. ...Thanks.

DANNY. You're so pretty.

ANA. Are you gonna kiss me?

DANNY. Do you want me to?

ANA. I don't know.

DANNY. 'Kay.

> *(He kisses her.)*

> *(She kisses him back.)*

> *(It gets intense.)*

> *(She moves backward onto the bed. He climbs on top of her. It all moves quickly, desperately, a little frantic, awkward, animal.)*

> *(She sucks in a breath.)*

Okay?

ANA. *(Small.)* ...Yup.

> *(And then it is quickly over.)*

> *(He rolls off of her. He breathes hard, puts his hands over his face for a moment. And looks at the ceiling.)*

> *(She looks down, wipes herself off with part of the sheet, then sits up.)*

> *(He looks to the side. Blood on the sheets.)*

DANNY. Oh shit, was that your first...

ANA. Yeah.

DANNY. *(Sitting up.)* Oh.

You okay?

ANA. Yup.

> *(She nods to him.)*

> *(She nods over and over. He puts a hand on her shoulder.)*

DANNY. I'm gonna get us out of here, okay?

ANA. *(Nodding.)* 'Kay.

    (A shift.)

^^^^^^^^^^

(**ANA** *sits on the edge of her rumpled bed.*
DANNY *lies across it. He wakes.*)

DANNY. What time is it?

ANA. ...Close to eleven.

DANNY. *(Rubbing his face.)* Euuughh fuck I feel like ass.

ANA. Well you were pretty wasted, so.

DANNY. Yeahhhh.

(*He looks around her room.*)

So this is college, huh?

ANA. Yup.

DANNY. Pretty shitty.

ANA. Yeah, well all dorms are shitty. Especially freshman dorms.

DANNY. Yeah, I guess so. No, I mean, you've made it look nice.

(*He looks at her.*)

Thanks for letting me crash here.

ANA. You're welcome.

DANNY. I reeeeally shouldn't have been driving, / so –

ANA. Yeah, I know. Your keys are over there.

DANNY. Okay. Are you trying to get rid of me?

ANA. No, I'm just – telling you where they are. I had to pry them out of your hands last night.

DANNY. Aw. Well thanks for looking out for me.

ANA. Sure.

DANNY. You're sweet.

> *(He rubs his face. She glances at him.)*

ANA. Are you okay?

DANNY. Uhhhh. My head hurts pretty bad.

ANA. You were pretty messed up last night.

DANNY. Yeahhh.

ANA. Do you remember anything?

DANNY. I dunno, I / guess?

ANA. Okay.

DANNY. I remember talking to you. I remember driving here. Why?

ANA. You said some pretty scary stuff, I wasn't sure if –.

DANNY. Aw, were you worried?

ANA. I mean...yeah, Danny. It was pretty bad.

DANNY. But you calmed me down, didn't you?

> *(He touches her hair, then stands up, stretches. She looks away.)*

ANA. I'm gonna go take a shower.

> *(She gets up and grabs her shower caddy.)*

DANNY. Do you have somewhere you have to be or something?

ANA. Yeah, I've got a class, so / I need to get ready.

DANNY. On a Saturday?

ANA. Yeah. I mean, it's a study group, but I need to be there.

DANNY. Okay, I was gonna say, we could go eat something somewhere?

ANA. I...yeah, I should really go to this thing.

DANNY. Come on...they shouldn't make you do school shit on Saturdays.

ANA. They're not making me. Your keys are over there. Try to be quiet when you go because we're not supposed to have unauthorized guests in here and you didn't sign in / or whatever.

DANNY. Jesus, okay.

(She heads toward the door.)

Hey! Ana.

...Sorry if I did something that wasn't – that you weren't into last night.

I was really drunk, / so.

ANA. Yup, you were.

DANNY. Are you mad at me?

ANA. No, I just really need to shower.

DANNY. You seem pissed.

ANA. I just really want to shower.

DANNY. Want company?

ANA. Danny.

DANNY. Just asking.

ANA. *(Turning to him.)* I can't be the only one calming you down, like – / what if I'm not around?

DANNY. I know that –

ANA. Okay, just – if I'm not around, you gotta be able to like – just – what if I'm not around / and like

DANNY. What do you mean? Where are you going?

ANA. I don't know! I just –

>   *(She shakes her head several times.)*

DANNY. *(Going to her.)* Yo – yo – hey – I had a weird night but I'm good, okay?

ANA. ...'Kay.

DANNY. I'm good.

>   *(The door opens, darkness beyond.* **DANNY** *disappears through it.)*

^^^^^^^^^^

(**ANA** *in her room at a Writers' Retreat.*)

(*A knock on the door. She stiffens. Another knock.*)

ANA. ...Hello?

STEVEN. Hi! It's Steven. I, / um...

ANA. Oh.

STEVEN. Sorry, I brought you – some food since you –

(**ANA** *opens the door.*)

Since you missed dinner.

Hi.

ANA. Hi.

STEVEN. Are you feeling okay?

ANA. Yes. Why?

STEVEN. Just because you missed dinner, I thought maybe you weren't feeling well.

ANA. I'm fine.

STEVEN. Oh. Okay. Well I don't know if you want any of this, but I just grabbed you a few / things, so...

ANA. Thanks. That's nice of you.

STEVEN. Yeah, of course.

(*He looks past her to the rumpled bed.*)

Oh no, I'm sorry, did I wake you up?

ANA. Nope.

STEVEN. Oh, okay, good.

ANA. Sometimes I work in bed.

STEVEN. Oh man, really? I'd fall right asleep. I have to stand the whole time I'm writing.

ANA. You never sit?

STEVEN. If I sit, then inevitably I'll put my head down on the desk and fall asleep. It's too tempting.

ANA. Ah.

STEVEN. So I have a standing desk. And truly terrible lower back pain.

ANA. Right.

STEVEN. I think maybe I'm not standing with the best posture – but I do get a shit-ton done, / so –

ANA. Oh, all right then.

STEVEN. It's a trade I'm willing to make.

ANA. Sure.

STEVEN. *(Holding out the food.)* Is any of this appealing to you? If not I'll – I can put it back in the kitchen, or I'll eat it later or / something.

ANA. Uhh sure. Thanks.

STEVEN. I just thought, there's no more meals till the morning and maybe you'd regret not eating now, so...

(She puts the plate on her desk.)

ANA. Thanks, I appreciate it.

STEVEN. I mean I know I always get hungry again around ten or eleven, so I've been squirreling away those cinnamon rolls from breakfast in my room.

ANA. Ah!

STEVEN. Fully iced. And buttered.

ANA. Wow, that sounds – decadent. You're not attracting bugs?

STEVEN. Oh no, I am. But that's just added protein.

ANA. Mm.

STEVEN. That is gross, I'm so / sorry.

ANA. Yes it is.

STEVEN. I'm so sorry.

In full disclosure, there are some bugs in my room, but I don't think they're in it for the cinnamon rolls.

ANA. What are they in it for?

STEVEN. Uhhh, my flesh.

ANA. Ah.

STEVEN. I feel like they should have warned all the writers we might get eaten alive while we're here.

ANA. Hm…

STEVEN. Pretty sure something is hiding in my room and eating me at night.

ANA. Mmm…that sounds like bed bugs.

STEVEN. NO. Oh no! I meant – no, I just meant some asshole mosquitos, / oh no!

ANA. Well, where are your bites?

STEVEN. I hope you know I would never approach you if I thought I had bed bugs.

ANA. Well thank you, / that's…

STEVEN. Oh – God. No! If I thought that you thought that I had bed bugs I would kill myself. I / would seriously…

ANA. Don't say that.

STEVEN. I'm – / what?

ANA. That's not funny.

STEVEN. I'm – sorry. Sorry.

> (*He glances at her. She looks back toward her bed for a moment.*)

These are my bites.

> (*He rolls up his pants, showing her his legs.*)

ANA. Oh holy Christ.

STEVEN. It's bad isn't it?

ANA. Jesus H. Christ.

STEVEN. I know, it's –

ANA. That's bad.

STEVEN. I know, it's! – / I told you –

ANA. That's really bad.

STEVEN. They're eating me / alive.

ANA. You need to put something on – all that.

STEVEN. Like what?

ANA. I don't know – calamine lotion? A – plaster cast? Cover that shit up!

STEVEN. Eugh, I know, I'm hideous. I'm –. Really gross.

ANA. You might have Zika.

STEVEN. (*Laughing.*) Wow! – Wow, I forgot about Zika.

ANA. It causes severe birth defects.

STEVEN. Yes!, I – I / remember now.

ANA. So don't get anyone pregnant.

STEVEN. Wow, that's horrible.

ANA. Just / saying.

STEVEN. You're a horrible person.

ANA. Yes.

(*A pause. She looks over her shoulder at the food on her desk.*)

Okay, well thanks for the food.

STEVEN. You're welcome. I'll leave you be. But IIIII willlll... I'll see you at breakfast?

ANA. We'll see.

STEVEN. ...Is there a reason you didn't come to dinner?

ANA. Um.

STEVEN. I know the socializing can be a lot.

ANA. Yeah, it's not really my thing.

STEVEN. I get that.

ANA. Do you? You seem to thrive at that part.

STEVEN. Oh well...that's because I'm sad and desperate for people to like me.

ANA. Ah, / okay.

STEVEN. And I like making people laugh. Which is maybe the less pathetic side of it.

ANA. Mm.

STEVEN. Or – maybe it's not.

ANA. Well take the Zika joke if you want it.

STEVEN. Oh, thank you so much.

ANA. Enjoy.

STEVEN. Thanks. Thank you. Do you think people will still get it? I feel like Covid obliterated Zika.

ANA. Okay, then don't take it.

STEVEN. No! – No, I'll still take it. Thank you.

Well, sorry, I'll leave now.

(He turns to go but stops himself.)

Eugh, except I'd be remiss if I didn't tell you that I loved your book. I loved it.

ANA. Oh, thank you.

STEVEN. I – it meant a lot to me. More than I can describe to you.

ANA. Thanks.

STEVEN. I couldn't read another book for months after that. Partly because I was utterly devastated, but also… I just – I didn't want to read anything else. I couldn't – it felt like I would be cheating on your characters. They really stayed with me. I wanted them to stay with me.

ANA. Hm. Well, thank you.

STEVEN. Are you working on a new book?

ANA. Supposed to be. That's why I'm here.

STEVEN. *(Staring at her.)* I can't wait to read it.

(She looks up at him, then away.)

I'm finally going to go back to my room now.

ANA. Sounds good.

(He goes to the door.)

STEVEN. Let the flesh-eating commence.

ANA. Steven.

STEVEN. Yeah?

ANA. I was working. That's why I didn't come to dinner.

STEVEN. Oh – / right.

ANA. Because I'm here to work. Just work. That's it.

STEVEN. Of course.

ANA. Have a good night.

STEVEN. Yeah – you too.

> *(He glances at her, gives a small nod, then retreats through the open door. She turns and looks at the bed.)*

^^^^^^^^^^^

(**DANNY** *in the doorway.*)

DANNY. Who was that guy?

ANA. What guy?

DANNY. The guy – that guy you were dancing with?

ANA. Were you spying on me?

DANNY. You were out there for everyone to see, weren't you? I didn't have to be spying to see your ass all up on him.

ANA. Euuughh Danny.

DANNY. Are you guys together?

ANA. I was dancing with him because it was a party and I was actually trying to have fun. We're not, like – / dating or whatever.

DANNY. Okay, well pretty sure he was getting off on you.

ANA. Okay, well, great.

DANNY. That doesn't bother you? That some dude you barely know is getting off on you.

ANA. No it doesn't.

DANNY. Ohhhh, so you like him?

ANA. We're in like one class together, I don't – we don't really know each other.

DANNY. But you like him.

ANA. I mean, I think he's smart.

DANNY. Right.

ANA. And why were you there?

DANNY. I'm allowed to go to a bar aren't I?

ANA. Yeah, sure, but, *that* bar? It's nowhere near your work or your apartment or – / anything, it's –

DANNY. And it's too nice for some dumbass like me. Right?

ANA. No.

DANNY. I know everyone in there was thinking who's this townie dipshit?

ANA. No they weren't.

DANNY. I know how people look at me Ana, don't tell me I don't know. I know.

ANA. Okay.

DANNY. Everyone in that place was thinking, who is this dumb piece of shit?

ANA. I don't think anyone was / thinking that, but, whatever.

DANNY. Like who is this guy, coming into our college bar?

ANA. I think everyone was just wondering why you were being such an asshole.

DANNY. I saw how they looked at me.

ANA. Yeah because you were being an asshole!

DANNY. I was drinking, don't you people drink?

ANA. Who is you people?

DANNY. You smart people.

ANA. Oh Jesus, Danny – Everyone was looking at you because you were loud jond and – out of control. That's why they were looking at you. Because you were acting like a scary fucking asshole, okay? They were scared of you.

(**DANNY** *sits on her bed, deflated.*)

DANNY. ...I am smart, you know.

ANA. I know you are.

DANNY. I'm actually – like I got pretty good grades and everything. I was smartest kid in my class for like – a while, like – / seriously, I was.

ANA. I'm – yeah, I didn't say you weren't smart.

DANNY. But you think it, don't you?

ANA. No.

DANNY. You always thought I was a dumbass, you never, no one ever, like gave me a fucking chance – and you would gang up against me – with *him*, like, "oh Ana, you have to help James with his math because Danny's too stupid,"/ and like –

ANA. I – okay, I never thought you were stupid.

DANNY. But then why did you just go along with it? – Like you never said anything, you just –

ANA. What are you / talking about?!

DANNY. You just went and did homework with James and you never said, like, you never even gave me a chance to do it!

ANA. Oh Jesus.

DANNY. What? What?!

ANA. I was just trying to *survive* Danny – I was trying to keep your dad from – going off, I didn't know you were upset about any of that.

DANNY. Well I was.

ANA. Well I'm sorry, I didn't know.

DANNY. *(Rubbing his eyes.)* Eughh fuck, whatever.

ANA. I'm sorry.

DANNY. *(Holding his hands over his eyes.)* Fuck it FUCK IT never mind, I'm just – I don't know why I care so much, you know?

I don't know why.

ANA. Danny. I know you're smart.

> (**DANNY** *nods several times, looking at her,*
> *then turns away.*)

DANNY. So what's his name?

ANA. What?

DANNY. The guy, that guy.

ANA. Why?

DANNY. Because if you like him so much I want to know about him.

ANA. I don't like him that much.

DANNY. No?

ANA. No. And this was like only the second time I've gone out to party with people *ever*, so – and I don't like anyone. I'm not looking for – that.

DANNY. What are you looking for?

ANA. I only have a year left here, I just want to finish school. And if I'm not working then...yeah, I just want to be sleeping. I'm tired.

DANNY. You like me.

ANA. Sure.

DANNY. Or you did.

ANA. I'm just trying to graduate and get a good job, / that's all I'm trying to do.

DANNY. Or I thought you did I guess.

ANA. ...Danny.

DANNY. Why don't you like me anymore?

ANA. I do, I just don't want to do – I told you I don't want to do that anymore.

DANNY. I know, I know.

I miss you though. That's why I came to the bar – I just miss seeing you.

ANA. Okay.

DANNY. I really miss seeing you.

ANA. Thanks, that's nice.

DANNY. …That's nice. Yeah.

> *(He covers his face for a moment. He uncovers it.)*

I got us out of there, you know?

ANA. I know.

DANNY. He was gonna – who knows what he was gonna fucking do to you.

ANA. I know, I –. Yeah.

DANNY. But I got us out of there.

ANA. Yeah. You did. I know.

> *(She nods, looking down.)*

DANNY. Eugh FUCK, my head hurts so bad.

ANA. Yeah?

DANNY. Just throbbing, like – eugh.

ANA. …Hey, I don't think you should drive.

DANNY. What?

ANA. You shouldn't be driving home.

> *(She leads him over to the bed.)*

Here.

DANNY. What's this?

ANA. You should sleep it off.

DANNY. Yeah? Here?

ANA. Yes.

(He touches a lock of her hair.)

DANNY. …You're sweet.

ANA. Just go to sleep, okay? Here.

(She pulls down the blankets for him. He climbs into bed. She sits next to him.)

DANNY. Will you do the thing?

ANA. Yeah.

(She rubs her thumbs in circles on his temples.)

DANNY. That feels so good.

ANA. Good.

(He wraps his arms around her. She stares rigidly at the door.)

*(**DANNY** disappears.)*

^^^^^^^^^^

(**STEVEN** *outside the door. He knocks.*)

STEVEN. Ana?

(**ANA** *sits on her bed, breathing. Trying to breathe. She puts a pillow over her face. Another knock.*)

Ana?

ANA. *(From inside the pillow.)* ...What?

STEVEN. Ana?

ANA. *(Dropping pillow.)* ...What?

(She throws the pillow.)

STEVEN. Hey. It's just me.

ANA. Who's me?

STEVEN. Sorry – Steven?

ANA. Go away you have Zika.

STEVEN. *(A small laugh.)* Oh Jesus!, Right! Okay!

(A tiny pause.)

It's not contagious?

ANA. What do you want?

STEVEN. Uhhhhh can I tell your face?

ANA. Why?

STEVEN. Because I feel weird out here saying vulnerable things loudly at, uh, at the door.

ANA. It's okay.

STEVEN. What?

ANA. Go ahead, the door is open to that.

STEVEN. The door is closed. Though.

ANA. Yeah, but it's receptive.

STEVEN. Ha! Okay.

Uhhhhh.

Well.

I just wanted to see if you were doing okay after that dinner, that whole conversation was – that all got a little weird and I was thinking maybe you weren't okay.

ANA. I'm fine.

STEVEN. ...All right!

Well.

Coooool. Then. I'll, uh.

ANA. Goodnight!

STEVEN. Goodnight!

(A pause. She rubs her face.)

(She stands up and starts clearing away some books scattered on her desk, but she's shaking a bit.)

(She pauses, stands upright, and taps her fingers on her chest in a pattern, one two three, one two three, one two three, and again, one two three, one two three, one two three, and again. She exhales.)

(She inhales.)

(She exhales.)

(She peers at the door.)

ANA. You're still out there aren't you?

STEVEN. Yeah?

ANA. What are you doing?

STEVEN. I don't know.

IIIIII wanted to make sure you were okay.

ANA. Yes, I told you I'm fine.

STEVEN. Yup, you did. And I should take you at your word and go away now... After I tell you that I'm sorry. I feel like that whole conversation at dinner got started and I was just going along with it because Sam is usually really funny and usually so benign and I usually enjoy his stories, and I've found Connor to be pretty cool thus far, but then he – man, I don't know, when he started saying all that stuff I should have said something – I should have spoken up or something, but I was just, I don't know, well, I was a coward I guess. I was cowardly. And I'm sorry. On behalf of everyone.

(She opens the door a crack.)

ANA. No, you're sorry on behalf of you. You don't speak for everyone.

STEVEN. Okay, yeah, you're right. I'm very sorry on behalf of me. And those other dicks might just be dicks?

ANA. Mmhmm.

STEVEN. I'm sorry.

ANA. This is why I don't like to go to dinner.

STEVEN. Are you okay?

ANA. You *have* stop asking me that – I'm not some weakass flower that faints every time some privileged guy says something completely fucking ignorant, okay?

STEVEN. Of course. Yes. I would never in a – in thousands of centuries think you were weakass. Or a flower. You're way too formidable for that.

Um. But I did bring you these since you left the table before they put them out.

(He hands her something wrapped in a napkin.)

And they are, I'm not just trying to be cheery here, really fucking good.

ANA. You really feel the need to feed me.

STEVEN. I…yeah, I really do. Not totally sure why that is, could probably unpack that, but let's not.

Mostly I just don't think you should miss out. They're cookies.

ANA. I see that.

STEVEN. I took a guess that you'd want three. But I brought about seven more back to my room, so if you want more…

ANA. You're only gonna bring more bugs on yourself.

STEVEN. Oh I surrendered to them last week. They've built a whole civilization, there's a whole hierarchy now, and I am their prisoner.

ANA. They like sugar.

STEVEN. Well me too, so we understand / each other.

ANA. I tried one of those cinnamon rolls you like. They are cloyingly sweet.

STEVEN. Oh, that's nothing. I put five packets of sugar in my coffee.

ANA. Oh God.

STEVEN. And I drink a lot of coffee, so. Yeahhh, we were denied all other things worth having growing up, so sugar became my vice.

ANA. What things?

STEVEN. Uhh, well. I was raised Mormon. So. A lot of things.

ANA. Whoooooooa.

STEVEN. Yeahhhhhh.

ANA. And you're not now?

STEVEN. Uhhhhh. I'm a journalist. And I found it hard to be both things, or to – hold both things.

And...then of course there was a lot about the belief system that I can't – I couldn't – get past.

ANA. Right.

STEVEN. But there are also things that – linger. Parts of it that I loved. That I still love.

ANA. Hm.

STEVEN. Catholic?

ANA. Why?

STEVEN. Because of your book, I just thought...

ANA. Mm, for a time. I went to church twice a week with my mom when I was a kid. But then we stopped.

STEVEN. Why?

ANA. She married this. Guy. And he wasn't into it.

STEVEN. He made you stop going?

ANA. Pretty much. Yup.

STEVEN. How?

ANA. What do you mean how?

STEVEN. He was just like, "Errr – if I find out you went to church, I'll stop seeing you?"

ANA. No, it was more like, "If I turn around one Wednesday or Sunday and you're not here to help me with my boys and cook and clean and do things for me, then I might beat the shit out of you, or I might not, but I'm definitely gonna keep you guessing."

STEVEN. Oh no.

ANA. So. With fear. Is how.

STEVEN. Ana.

ANA. And then she died, / so.

STEVEN. Oh I'm so sorry.

ANA. So definitely no more church then.

STEVEN. You stayed with him?

ANA. Yeah, I had nowhere to go. And no money, / so.

STEVEN. For how long?

ANA. Until a breaking point was reached.

(He looks at her, really stares at her. She looks back at him.)

I don't want to be looked at like that.

STEVEN. Oh – I'm –

ANA. Like that.

STEVEN. Okay. I will look over here.

ANA. I need to write. I've got two good hours left in my brain, / so.

STEVEN. Of course. Of course.

ANA. I want to take advantage of the time. Thanks for the cookies.

STEVEN. Bahhhh but I want to ask you so many questions.

ANA. I should work.

STEVEN. Can I ask you just – two more questions?

ANA. One.

STEVEN. One. Okay.

Do you still believe in God?

And it doesn't have to be Catholic God, it could be any – anything, someone or something watching you? Seeing you?

(She looks at him for a moment before responding.)

ANA. No.

STEVEN. Why?

ANA. That's two questions.

STEVEN. You're right.

(A pause.)

ANA. Goodnight.

STEVEN. Okay. Goodnight.

See you at breakfast?

ANA. Goodnight.

STEVEN. I hope to see you at breakfast.

ANA. Goodnight.

(He nods and steps into the doorway. He gives a small wave, then disappears.)

(She stares at the door. Puts her hands on her hips. The drops her arms by her side again. She shakes her head, shaking something off. Then she turns back toward the work on her desk and lays her hands on it.)

^^^^^^^^^

(**DANNY** *in the doorway.*)

DANNY. Must be something good.

ANA. Ohmygod! – You scared the shit out of me.

DANNY. Whatever you're reading.

ANA. What?

DANNY. Must be something good. I've been standing here for two minutes, you didn't even notice.

ANA. Well, that's – creepy Danny.

DANNY. Why?

ANA. You should have said something.

DANNY. Hi Ana.

(*He has a cut under his bruised eye. And a crudely-bandaged hand.*)

ANA. What happened to you?

DANNY. Eh...just some dumb asshole.

ANA. What happened?

DANNY. He said some shit to me, I said some shit back, he hit me, I – put my fist through his car window.

ANA. God – Danny.

DANNY. So now my hand's fucked up.

ANA. Maybe you should go to the doctor.

DANNY. Why? So they can tell me I have a black eye and a fucked-up hand? I know / that.

ANA. But is there still glass in it?

DANNY. Pretty sure I got it all out.

ANA. It could get infected.

DANNY. You worried about me?

ANA. No, I'm just – telling you it looks bad.

DANNY. I think you're worried about me.

ANA. You should go to the doctor.

DANNY. You're worried about me.

ANA. I mean yeah, I'd rather you not die of gangrene or whatever.

DANNY. Don't think that's how I'll be dying, hon.

What are you reading over there?

ANA. Nothing.

DANNY. What is it?

(She tucks her pages away.)

ANA. Just something for a class.

DANNY. What's the class?

ANA. Why?

DANNY. Woo – you're being all secretive.

ANA. No I'm not, I'm just...

DANNY. I can't ask you questions about your life?

ANA. You can.

DANNY. I can't be interested in what you're doing here?

ANA. How'd you get in this time?

DANNY. What?

ANA. The security guy didn't stop you?

DANNY. Didn't see any security guy. One of your friends let me in.

ANA. What friend?

DANNY. I don't know, skinny girl, said she knew you. What are you worried about?

ANA. Nothing, just – there's supposed to be someone at the door, to like –

DANNY. Keep people like me out.

ANA. There's just supposed to be a security guy and I'm just...wondering where that guy is.

DANNY. I don't know, Ana, man probably took a break. So tell me what's this thing.

ANA. It's just something for my writing class.

DANNY. Oh, like – a story?

ANA. Kind of. We're making these things called "chapbooks," like a final – a collection of our writing from the semester, and then we each read an excerpt for a bunch of people, like as a final – event for the seniors in the department.

DANNY. Can I read it?

ANA. No.

DANNY. Why?

ANA. It's not finished yet. And it's private.

DANNY. What's it about?

ANA. I don't know, a lot of things.

DANNY. Like...what?

ANA. I don't know, I'm still working on it.

DANNY. Like, what, like kings and queens and dragons and shit, / or is it like –

ANA. No, no, it's nonfiction.

DANNY. Okay.

ANA. So...it's about me, I guess.

DANNY. Why can't I read it?

ANA. Why do you want to?

DANNY. Because I want to. Because I'm interested, can't /
I be interested?

ANA. No, I know, I just don't want anyone reading it yet.

DANNY. Am I in it?

ANA. No. Can we stop talking / about it?

DANNY. It's about your life and I'm not in it?

ANA. I mean, a brief mention maybe, but it doesn't like, /
it's not about that.

DANNY. A brief mention.

ANA. It's more about me, and my mom, and like – our life
before.

DANNY. It's about your mom?

ANA. Yes.

DANNY. What about her?

ANA. Just, like, I don't know, how we used to go to church
and, I don't know, the way she – everything, how she
looked, how she smelled, her voice, / just...

DANNY. Yeah, she always smelled like food.

ANA. What?

DANNY. I don't mean that bad, I mean, like, she was
always cooking something, she smelled like, like,
onions and vinegar and oil and like – good food.

ANA. Yeah.

DANNY. We were hungry all the time before you guys
came. James and me were like, eating cereal out of a
box with no milk, whatever trash I could get from the
7-11. Then he'd get mad at *us* when he'd come home
and there was no food.

ANA. Yeah.

DANNY. But then your mom's food tasted so good.

ANA. I know.

DANNY. I mean, maybe it was because we were so fucking hungry, but I remember feeling like I could just eat forever. Like I could sit at that table and never stop eating.

ANA. Me too.

DANNY. …She was nice to me. She always used to, um.

ANA. What?

DANNY. She'd just – when she was talking to us, she'd sometimes just pat the top of my head, like pet my hair kinda, but not weird, it was just – nice.

ANA. Yeah.

DANNY. She was really nice. I never got why she wanted to be with him.

ANA. She didn't. She just got trapped.

DANNY. Hm.

ANA. And she was afraid. Of what he'd do. She was terrified.

> *(He nods.* **ANA** *inhales. Her phone buzzes twice over by her bed. She goes over to look at it.)*

DANNY. *(Edging closer to the desk.)* Who's that?

> *(She texts.)*

ANA. *(Texting.)* Just – a friend from my class.

> *(***DANNY*** *picks up the pages from the folder on on her desk.)*

DANNY. *(Reading the pages.)* Are you going out or something?

ANA. *(Texting.)* Uhh, we're supposed to – yeah, we're meeting up before dinner...

DANNY. A friend like a guy or a friend like a girl?

ANA. A girl, Danny, god.

> *(She looks up.)*

What are you doing? – No!

DANNY. What?! I just want to see it for a second!

> *(She tries to get the pages out of his hands.)*

ANA. No! Danny! I said no!

DANNY. I'm just! – Just let me!

ANA. STOP – Give it back!

DANNY. I just want to see it, / especially –

ANA. DANNY, Stop!

> *(He holds his arm out, keeping her at bay.)*

DANNY. *(Holding her at bay.)* ESPECIALLY if I'm in it for a "brief mention," don't I deserve to read the part about me...?

ANA. Danny, please.

DANNY. *(Reading.)* Just let me read...

ANA. Danny –

DANNY. Just – shut up for a second!

> *(He reads.)*

> *(She collapses, sitting on the bed.)*

> *(He stops reading. He nods over and over.)*

You were always good at stories. Remember the ones you used to tell James?

ANA. …Yeah.

DANNY. He loved that. I loved that. I used to listen at the door when you would put him to bed, just to hear whatever story you made up.

ANA. You did?

DANNY. Yeah, you were so good at it.

(He looks down at her pages.)

…Is this how you think of me?

ANA. I'm – it's just. For a class, it's not…

DANNY. Is it though?

ANA. I don't know.

DANNY. Because…that just makes me wanna die.

ANA. Danny.

(He sits next to her on the bed.)

(He covers his eyes for a moment.)

DANNY. I want to die. Euuuughhhh.

ANA. I mean, this has always been pretty messed up, hasn't it?

DANNY. Why?

ANA. You know why. You know why.

DANNY. It doesn't feel messed up / to me –

ANA. Well I'm pretty sure this is pretty fucked up.

DANNY. Being with you is the only time I don't feel messed up.

ANA. Well that's…really fucked up Danny. This whole thing is fucked up.

(She rubs her eyes. He watches her.)

DANNY. You're going to read this in front of people?

ANA. I don't know.

DANNY. Are you?

ANA. Yes, / but just a part –

DANNY. In front of all your friends and your, / all your little –

ANA. I don't know what part I'll read. It's just for my class, / it's –

DANNY. Fuck Ana. Fuck. Fuck fuck fuck.

(He picks up a vase on her bedside table and hurls it at the wall. It shatters.)

Fucking fuck fuck! Fuck you.

(He paces the room. She scuttles back on the bed.)

ANA. Danny –

DANNY. Fucking fuck fuck.

(He picks up a shard of glass, he cuts himself with it.)

ANA. What are you – Danny! – What are you doing?

DANNY. This is what you make me do.

(He cuts himself again.)

ANA. Danny, stop!

DANNY. *(Holding up his bleeding arms.)* This is what you make me do!

This is what you make me do.

This is what you make me do.

*(**ANA** runs to her door and screams into the dark hallway.)*

ANA. Help! I need help! Someone help! I need help!

(She goes to him, kneeling, he looks up at her with a sad smile, and then he disappears, as though falling through a hole in the floor.)

^^^^^^^^^^

STEVEN. / Are you okay?!

ANA. Fucking fuck fuck.

STEVEN. I heard a crash, are you –

> (**ANA** *kneels on the floor, shards of a broken vase around her.*)

ANA. *(Gathering shards.)* Shit.

STEVEN. *(Looking for a trash can.)* Oh no, wait – don't don't touch – be careful, hold on. Are you okay?

ANA. I'm just going to pick up the big pieces.

STEVEN. No, no, wait – I'll help you. But I saw a thing in the closet – like a dustbuster-y thing – just wait, I want to help you.

> (**ANA** *sits back, looking at her hands.*)

Did you cut yourself?

ANA. No.

STEVEN. Okay – I'll be right back. Don't touch it!

> *(He leaves. She looks at the floor, then pulls a wastebasket over.)*

> *(He reappears with a dustbuster.)*

Mwah-ha! This should help us.

ANA. I'm just going to get the big pieces first.

STEVEN. Yeah, of course – And then we'll dust-bust the shit out of this little stuff.

(*They start gingerly picking up big shards of glass and dropping them in the wastebasket.*)

What happened?

ANA. I broke a vase.

STEVEN. In a fit of rage, or?

ANA. Maybe.

STEVEN. Really?

ANA. Yeah, why not?

STEVEN. I don't know. Good question. Were you in a fit of rage?

ANA. (*Shrugging.*) It fell.

It shattered.

STEVEN. Hm.

(*They gather up a few more pieces.*)

ANA. I think we've got what we can get.

STEVEN. Time to dust-bust this shit?

ANA. I guess so. Here –

STEVEN. No way, I live to dust-bust.

ANA. Why?

STEVEN. It's satisfying in a way that few things in adult life are.

ANA. I can / do it –

STEVEN. Please let me dust-bust the shards of your vase. It would be my honor.

ANA. ...Fine.

(*He does a small bow, then dust-busts. She stands and watches for a moment, then goes to put on her shoes.*)

STEVEN. Okay. I think we're good here.

Maybe just don't walk around barefoot in this general area.

ANA. I won't.

> *(She moves the wastebasket back under her desk.)*

Thank you.

STEVEN. Of course. I'm just glad you didn't cut yourself.

> *(She studies him for a brief moment.)*

ANA. Your bites look better.

STEVEN. *(Looking down at his legs.)* Thanks! – Yeah. I put some Cortisone on them. Also I've been spraying my naked body in Deep Woods Off! every night before bed, / so...

ANA. *(Cringing.)* Woof.

STEVEN. So that's helping.

ANA. I'm glad. Though, that is horrifying, / but – I'm glad it's helping.

STEVEN. I know, I'm already regretting telling you that.

ANA. That stuff makes me want to jump in a shower immediately, I cannot –

STEVEN. No, I know, and it's probably making me radioactive, too, but...

ANA. But. It works.

STEVEN. It does.

...Can I ask you some more questions?

ANA. It depends what they are.

STEVEN. I don't know exactly what they are yet.

ANA. Then no.

STEVEN. Well – wait, now – wait. What if we define distinct...general...themes?

ANA. Mm...

STEVEN. And then I'll base each question on one of those themes?

ANA. How many themes are you trying to have?

STEVEN. How many can I have?

ANA. Three.

STEVEN. Three? Okay. Three.

Okay. Okay.

Okay.

Okay.

Okay!

The themes will be: your childhood –

(To her shaking head.) – No?

ANA. We'll see.

STEVEN. Okay. Your childhood, tentatively, Your relationship to writing, and Your relationship to God.

ANA. *(Squinting at him.)* Mmmm...

STEVEN. Do you approve?

ANA. I'm also going to ask you questions.

STEVEN. Good. I hope so.

ANA. On similar or maybe different themes.

STEVEN. Well that's all-encompassing – the field is wide open then? For me?

ANA. Yup.

STEVEN. Mm... Okay. I accept.

ANA. I'll start.

STEVEN. Great.

ANA. Why are you fixated on / me?

STEVEN. Ooh. Th– I don't know if –. The word "fixated" kinda makes me shudder a little.

ANA. Why?

STEVEN. It makes it seem like my interest in you is more about obsession than...interest.

ANA. Is it not?

STEVEN. Obsessive?

ANA. Yes.

STEVEN. I don't know. I don't think so. It doesn't feel that way to me, does it feel that way to you?

ANA. I haven't decided. You are persistent.

STEVEN. That's true.

ANA. So. One might call your interest obsessive.

STEVEN. If it feels that way to you, I am so sorry. I am very, very interested in you, that is true, but I did not mean for that to make you feel...anything weird.

ANA. Thanks.

STEVEN. I – do you want me to still answer the original question?

ANA. Yes.

STEVEN. Uhhhh I am interested in you because...well, I guess it started because I read your book and I found it to be an incredibly profound and exquisitely-crafted piece of writing. That I still think about all the time. And then I met you, here, I mean, here you are in this remote – farmhouse-y artist place – aaaaaand, I think you know this?, but you just carry so much behind your eyes, I mean…there are just worlds in there and then knowing that that book came out of you, I just – yeah, I want to ask you every question in the universe so I can know what you think about things.

(She nods a very small nod.)

…My turn?

ANA. I guess.

STEVEN. When did your childhood end?

ANA. (Laughing.) Jesus fuck!

STEVEN. Is that an all-right question?

ANA. Uhhh, yeah, it's. Fine.

Um.

Officially the night I met the guy that became my stepfather. He came over for dinner. My mom cooked for him. And just the way he sat at that table, the way he ate, the way he looked at her, everything – the way he looked at me, talked to me. I understood that we were going to be tied to him because he had money and we didn't. I saw all the pieces of the rope start to come together that night, and I kinda knew why it was happening and also knew it was going to be really…that there would be consequences. I didn't have the words then, just, a deep, deep sick feeling.

STEVEN. How old were you?

ANA. Eleven.

STEVEN. And when your mom died?

ANA. Fourteen.

STEVEN. Hm. And then when…what was the breaking point with him?

ANA. You've blown through all of your questions.

STEVEN. Oh shit. Can we – we could categorize those as follow-up questions that don't count toward the original three?

ANA. We'll see.

When did you flee Mormonism?

STEVEN. Officially? Or in my heart?

ANA. Both.

STEVEN. Officially in the middle of college. I left Brigham Young during sophomore year and ran east.

But in my heart...uhh... I'd say our relationship started unraveling at fourteen or fifteen.

ANA. Why?

STEVEN. Uuum. In the Mormon church you start confessing your sins to the Bishop when you're twelve. You go in a room with a guy who is not behind a curtain, who is not trained, who is not paid, who is chosen by the church to basically be a volunteer pastor for a short period of time. So you go in a closed room and talk about all of your sexual sins. They ask you questions like, What do you fantasize about? Did you go to first base? Where did you put your hands? Did you like it?

ANA. Eugh.

STEVEN. Which...goes differently for every person, depending on who your Bishop is, but I had Chris, and Chris asked me all kinds of things I only later understood were, are, really, really wrong. And he... yeah, made me feel...

(He shakes his head.)

Sick. All the time. Dirty?

So...yeah. Closing myself in a room with an older man and telling him all the details of my sexual acts – or, even worse, in a way, my sexual thoughts kinda... I mean when I felt like he – they starting taking my thoughts from me, when I understood that they were starting to own my thoughts, *my thoughts*, that was – and that they were doing it to all of us, that they were willfully causing harm to all of us, that was when my whole being kinda...unraveled.

ANA. Hm.

STEVEN. I mean, the man never touched me, I was never touched, but – yeah, so I don't have any business being traumatized. But to this day, I still – have trouble.

ANA. With.

STEVEN. With...sex stuff.

(**ANA** *nods several times.*)

ANA. What kind of trouble?

STEVEN. You're gonna get right in there, huh?

(She looks at him, unflinching.)

...Uhhh. I guess I. Have trouble not feeling some bit of shame after. Or sometimes during. I get that thing where I kind of separate from my body and I'm watching myself – do things, but my thoughts are like oh no, oh no, this probably isn't good, you're probably going to feel really bad after this – whole thing is over, oh no, oh no, et cetera. Et cetera.

ANA. And what about who you're with?

STEVEN. Uhhh well I've only ever been – fully been – with two women. And I think I hid my shame from them pretty well.

ANA. Really?

STEVEN. *(Laughing.)* ...No. I guess...probably, yeah, probably if I really think about it, which you're making me do, all the things that I thought broke us up were really just about me and my – sexual dread!, so... – Can I ask you a question now?

ANA. Okay.

STEVEN. Was your stepfather violent to you? Was / that what the...

ANA. He hit Danny. He beat the shit out of Danny. He never hit me. He threatened me but never followed through. But then he tried, um. Well my mother died of breast cancer. So one night he told me he needed to check me for lumps.

STEVEN. Oh no.

ANA. And when I said No he got so – he got really angry and he came / at me –

STEVEN. God god god.

ANA. But Danny pulled him off. Danny pulled him off and hit him with a lamp. / Knocked him out.

STEVEN. Whoa – oh God.

ANA. Then he dragged him down to the basement and... locked him in there, it was like a horror movie, he locked him in the basement – and we grabbed some things and left. I never went back to that house.

STEVEN. Who's Danny?

ANA. His older son. My – stepbrother.

STEVEN. Okay. So where did you go?

ANA. Uhhhh, well we took James, the younger one, to a friend's house, and then we, um. We lived in the car some, sometimes just random people would let us stay for a night or two. We did some homeless shelters but that was – honestly I preferred the car to some of those.

STEVEN. How long did this go on?

ANA. A year. Then Danny found us a place with a bunch of guys from work, but that was awful!, so I started sleeping over at school – there was this one English teacher that helped me out. So I slept in her office until I graduated.

STEVEN. Holy shit Ana.

How did you not – how did you not just fall off the face of the earth? I would not have survived any of that.

> *(She opens her hands, a gesture of not having an answer, or not having the words for an answer.)*

ANA. ...I had work, I had writing. That was a means of survival.

STEVEN. And so then, so, what happened to your – to Danny?

ANA. He, uhhh, killed himself. Shot himself in the head.

> *(***STEVEN***'s hands move quickly to his mouth.)*

...Yeah.

The same day I got into graduate school, weirdly enough.

He.

Uh.

Yeah, I don't know – I had school, I had my writing, and he didn't have that, he didn't have any of that, he didn't have anything, he only had me, I was it, and yeah, I don't know, I don't know.

STEVEN. Are you –

ANA. I don't know, it's. I don't know I don't know.

STEVEN. Okay.

ANA. I don't know I don't know.

STEVEN. ...What don't you know?

What don't you know?

ANA. ...He only had me. And – we – our relationship was really fucked up, so...

STEVEN. What do you mean?

ANA. I don't want to explain right now.

STEVEN. Okay.

ANA. But I hurt him. Badly. So.

STEVEN. But you were a kid. You were both – kids, right?

ANA. Didn't feel like a kid.

STEVEN. And I imagine...he hurt you too?

ANA. I think I'm done for tonight, okay?

STEVEN. Okay.

ANA. *(Looking around.)* I need to, um...um...

STEVEN. *(Getting up to go.)* Do you want me – here, I'll let you be / alone –

ANA. I'm just really tired.

STEVEN. Yeah yeah.

ANA. *(Covering her eyes, a weird laugh to herself.)* I'm so tired.

STEVEN. Yeah, of course.

> *(She stands, her hands over her eyes, shaking a tiny bit, frozen for several moments.)*

Hey.

Here.

Ana? Here.

(He goes to the bed and pulls the blankets back for her, gently guides her that way, without touching her. She follows, climbs into bed, almost like a child, wordless. She turns to the side, exhausted, hugging herself, her eyes closed. He pulls the blankets up and around her.)

(Then he goes slowly over toward the door. He hits the light switch and the room darkens. He quietly starts to leave.)

ANA. *(Her eyes still closed.)* Don't leave.

(He pauses, turns back to her.)

(He walks back toward her and slides himself down against the foot of the bedframe. He looks at her for a moment, then back out at the room.)

^^^^^^^^^

(*Very early morning, the sun only beginning to come up.* **ANA** *sleeps in a little heap.* **STEVEN** *lies asleep next to Ana's bed, his shirt or sweater balled up as a pillow.*)

(**JONAH** *appears next to the bed.*)

JONAH. (*Whispering.*) Ana.

A-*na*.

(*She stirs.*)

Ana!

(*She turns to him.*)

Are you awake?

ANA. (*Sitting up.*) Yes! – Are you awake?

JONAH. Oh I've been awake all night.

ANA. No you haven't.

JONAH. Yes I have! I totally / have!

ANA. No you haven't you / weirdo –

JONAH. *Yes* I have! – And you don't know because you were asleep!

ANA. Okay so were you just watching me all night?

JONAH. I mean I was looking at you, yeah.

ANA. For like seven hours straight?

JONAH. Yeah.

ANA. No you weren't you *weirdo* –

JONAH. *Yes* I was you – you –

ANA. You what?

JONAH. Never mind.

ANA. Nope, say it say it!

JONAH. Nothing, you're – I didn't mean anything!

ANA. No, say what you were gonna say, say what you were gonna say –

JONAH. I wasn't going to say anything!

ANA. You were gonna call me a name, I heard it, you were gonna –

JONAH. Okay! Jesus! Okay, I was just going to say I *have* been awake all night you crazy – *(She glares at him.)* – you crazy beautiful smart amazing girl that I – um.

ANA. What?

JONAH. That I love. So much I cannot possibly explain.

(She looks out at the room.)

ANA. I'm not a girl.

(He looks at her with tenderness.)

JONAH. Yes you are.

(She looks at him.)

ANA. Let's pretend we're at our twenty-year reunion.

JONAH. Whoa, okay, do we still know each other?

ANA. No.

JONAH. Aw.

ANA. Well we grew apart, it happens.

JONAH. That sucks.

ANA. Sorry.

JONAH. *(Shrugging.)* Eh, okay, so you're the one who got away who I'm still pining for?, / or –

ANA. Yeah! Yeah.

JONAH. 'Kay. *(A quick shift.)* Wow, hey, it's been a long time.

ANA. It has.

JONAH. Wow. Man. Hi.

ANA. Hi.

JONAH. You look great.

ANA. So do you.

JONAH. But you always looked great. Oh – thanks.

ANA. How are you?

JONAH. Good, I'm okay, I'm – yeah. Fine.

ANA. What are you up to?

JONAH. You know. Kinda floating. Waiting to see what's next. What about you?

ANA. Uhhh, just – working a lot, you know.

JONAH. Yeah, sure.

ANA. Trying to just work as much as I can.

JONAH. Right, right.

Well.

Listen, I – don't want to take up too much of your time, I just wanted to say that I don't really know what happened, but I'm really sorry if I ever did anything to hurt you, and I love you, and I just wish you well in all your endeavors, / so.

ANA. You didn't.

JONAH. What?

ANA. I – you didn't do anything wrong.

JONAH. Okay, I, just – we were so – together – and then all of a sudden you were – gone.

ANA. I know, I just, I don't know, things happened and I / couldn't –

JONAH. I thought I must have done something, I must have screwed up really bad or / something.

ANA. No no no, it wasn't you, it was just – things happened and I, I, I – lost that part of myself. I had to burn it or bury it or something –. Drop it down the well. Let it drown.

JONAH. What part?

ANA. The part that wanted to be touched. Like that. The way you touched me.

JONAH. Oh.

Is it gone for good do you think?

ANA. I think so.

JONAH. Oh no.

ANA. Yeah.

(They look at their hands.)

JONAH. ...What about how you touched me?

ANA. What?

JONAH. The part of you that wanted to touch me. That liked – touching me. Do you still have that?

ANA. I don't know.

JONAH. Maybe that's...maybe that will lead you somewhere.

*(**JONAH** glances to where **STEVEN** is curled up on the floor.)*

JONAH. Well I should probably go get some punch or something. But, uh – it was really good to see you.

ANA. Yeah. You too.

*(**JONAH** goes to the door, looks at her briefly, then disappears, closing the door.)*

*(**STEVEN** wakes with a start.)*

STEVEN. I fell asleep. I'm sorry.

ANA. *(Turning to **STEVEN**.)* That's okay.

*(**ANA** sits on the edge of the bed. **STEVEN** rubs his face, then slowly pulls himself up and sits on the edge of the bed near her.)*

STEVEN. What time is it?

ANA. Early, I think.

STEVEN. How long have you been up?

ANA. Not long.

STEVEN. ...'kay.

(He rubs his face.)

ANA. One question left.

STEVEN. What?

ANA. You have one question left.

STEVEN. *(A small laugh.)* Oh man, I'm – that's okay. I'll stop asking you things.

ANA. I want you to ask me.

STEVEN. I – Oh.

ANA. Ask me.

STEVEN. Okay.

ANA. "What is your relationship to God?"

STEVEN. …What is your relationship to God?

> (**ANA** *inhales.*)

ANA. I think. I think God is when you are truly, fully, in your body. When you have your thoughts and you have your body and they're somehow messily joined for a few seconds, even, like when you're a child and you're running through the cold air in the fall, and your chest hurts and you're cold but you're also sweating and you know you only have a few more minutes before someone calls you inside but you're just running until then and you feel absolutely completely fucking alive, or when you're with someone you trust, you truly trust, in your bones, you trust them and you're with them and every particle and every thought somehow connect into this breathing, beautiful, vibrating – vessel – when all the disparate parts of your body join each other in this exultant moment of of of – power – *that* is divine. That is God. And when I stopped being in my body. I lost God.

That's why I stopped believing.

> (*She turns to him.*)

And I feel – powerless. Powerless in the world. Like I'm walking around with no skin.

> (**STEVEN** *nods. He looks at her. She looks back out. He looks back out.*)

> (**STEVEN** *puts his hand halfway across the distance between them, his palm open on the bed.*)

STEVEN. …I'm just going to put my hand here.

If you want to hold it. Or just – hold onto something. It's – I'm just going to leave it here.

ANA. Okay.

STEVEN. And, also I think – um.

You wrote the most breathtaking book that I – that got into my bloodstream and curled up in my – I don't know, deep in my guts, certainly in my heart, and that I carry in me, and I'm just one little guy, there are, I know there are thousands of other people, whole, like, whole hurting human people carrying your words in them too. That's power. That you have. And I think that's God too.

ANA. Hm.

> *(She stares out for several moments. She slowly puts her hand on top of his.)*

Do you –. Can you still fantasize?

STEVEN. Uhhhhhh... You mean...about sexy stuff?

ANA. Yes.

STEVEN. Uhhhhhhhhhhhhhhhh yeah? There's definitely still shame lurking around some corners, but – I can sometimes...sometimes it's okay.

ANA. What happens? In the – in your fantasy?

STEVEN. Uhhhhhhhhh I mean it changes, it's – I don't know, it's – hm. Yikes.

ANA. General themes.

STEVEN. General themes, um...okay, uhhhhhhhh I'll just throw out some images / if that's okay?

ANA. Yeah.

STEVEN. Okay, so...being um, uhhhhh against a bedroom wall, uhhhhh, making out in the middle of an ocean, aaaand being in the woods, like deep in the woods, somewhere really far away and remote, on like a – bed of moss.

ANA. And who are you with?

STEVEN. *(Embarrassed.)* I don't know!

ANA. Is it always the same person?

STEVEN. No, no, well – I mean, it'll be one person for a while, whoever I'm, if there's someone – if I really like – a person, then – that person, uhh – will be the person for a period of time.

ANA. You like being out in the elements.

STEVEN. *(Laughing, hiding his face.)* Auugh yeah, I guess? Not the bedroom wall one, though, that one's…

ANA. What?

STEVEN. Quiet. Lamp-lit. Intimate, but…intense?

ANA. Hm.

STEVEN. Do – can you? Still fantasize?

ANA. I used to. When I was young, I had these elaborate – elaborate – I had a whole other fully-lived life in my head.

STEVEN. What happened in it?

ANA. Oh, I…well, my mom was still alive. And I had two sisters. I was the baby. All girls. And… I went to this boarding school? – somewhere in the – way far away, in the mountains somewhere, with this very overbearing dorm-parent. And I met this – boy, this funny, strange boy. Who was sad and so vulnerable. Kind. And I trusted him, like I really –. Truly trusted him.

(She laughs a small laugh.)

And touching was like – electricity. It was powerful.

STEVEN. Wow.

(She looks at their hands touching.)

ANA. Am I the person right now?

STEVEN. *(Closing his eyes.)* Uhhhhhhhh. I don't know if
I can answer that.

ANA. Why?

STEVEN. Because I want you to – feel safe.

ANA. Am I in the ocean?

STEVEN. No.

ANA. On the bed of moss?

STEVEN. Mmm No.

ANA. Hh. Bedroom wall then?

STEVEN. Ana.

I'm –

ANA. It's okay.

STEVEN. Um...

ANA. It's okay.

Come with me.

STEVEN. ...Okay.

> *(She stands, pulling him up. She leads him
> toward the wall. She gently pushes him up
> against it, one hand still holding his hand,
> the other on his chest.)*

ANA. Like this?

STEVEN. Um, yeah.

> *(She moves a little closer to him.)*

ANA. Like this?

STEVEN. ...Yeah.

> *(She moves her face closer to his.)*

ANA. Like this?

(He nods.)

(She touches him. She touches him. She touches him.)

Like that?

STEVEN. Yes.

ANA. Are you okay?

STEVEN. Yeah.

Are you okay?

ANA. ...Yes.

(She kisses him. He kisses her back. Their arms slowly wrap around each other, moving over and around each other, a kind of dance, and it's hot and beautiful and electric and alive. Vibrating. Exultant.)

(The light changes around them.)

∧∧∧∧∧∧∧∧

End of Play